MW00979250

©1994 Grandreams Limited.

Published by
Grandreams Limited
Jadwin House, 205/211 Kentish Town Road, London,
NW5 2JU.

Printed in Italy.

BW1-4

THE PIED PIPER
OF HAMELIN

Illustrated by Pam Storey.
Stories re-told by Grace De La Touche.

1

Once upon a time there was a town called Hamelin, on the banks of the River Weser.

The merchants of the town were successful in all their ventures and made lots of money. Their wives were mistresses of beautiful houses and they were more

than happy to spend the money their husbands made. This kept the shop-keepers in the town happy, as the merchants' wives delighted in holding parties and balls, picnics and luncheons to which many people were invited.

These happy events kept the dressmakers busy preparing outfits for every new occasion. The bakers were kept busy providing the bread and the cakes for the parties. The butchers and the grocers were busy - in fact the whole town was

very busy and very prosper-ous. Even the street clean-ers were kept busy, as the town council proudly kept the town as smart and as clean as possible.

Imagine the horror, therefore, when one day, a man ran into the council chambers, and screamed out, "A rat! I've just seen a rat! There's a rat in the street!"

The council and the Mayor stood up together. "A rat?" they asked. "Where?"

"It was going into a

hole in a wall, as clear as day!" cried the man.

"It's not possible," said the Mayor, dusting off his sleeve. "Hamelin is the cleanest town in the land. We don't have rats here."

"But it's true! I saw a rat!" insisted the man.

The councillors looked at each other in disbelief, each saying the same thing to himself, "There are no rats in Hamelin."

The man persisted, and eventually the councillors and the Mayor followed him. Outside, the man pointed to a hole in the side of a building. "It went in there," he said.

The councillors waited and watched. After a while, a whiskered nose peeped out of the hole, and the councillors gasped as they saw the beady eyes and the round ears of the rat.

"A rat!" cried the Mayor. "Get a cat!"

A cat was sent for, and was set to catch the rat. "That should do the trick," said the Mayor, dusting off his hands. "We can go home now. Our problem will

be over by morning." The councillors all nodded.

The next morning the cat had not caught the rat. And there was not just one rat. Rats were being seen all

over town! It was not a couple of rats, or ten rats - after a few days, it was thousands of rats! The once happy town of Hamelin was now very unhappy. The rats were destroying everything. They chewed their way into the houses, and into the cupboards in the houses. They ate the food in the cupboards in the kitchens, in the poorer houses as well as the rich merchants' houses.

They found their way into the wardrobes and drawers of the ladies of the town. They built nests in hats and scarves, had their babies in the nests and then even more rats ran around the town.

They chewed their way through doors and windows into the schools, making more nests in the desks and wastepaper bins. They chewed holes in books and paper.

There were not enough cats to catch the rats, and the rat-catchers could not keep up with all the reports! The situation was becoming hopeless.

The Mayor called a meeting at the town hall. He stood before the council - as a rat had chewed a hole in his chair! "There must be something we can do," he said. "Hamelin will be ruined if this continues."

But nobody had any ideas. This sort of thing had never happened before!

Within a few days of the first rat being seen, the people of the town had become desperate. They marched to the town hall. Coats had holes in, shoes were nibbled. Nobody had

anything that had not been touched by the rats!

"Mayor!" they called out. "You must do something! You and the councillors must find a way to drive out these rats!"

"I've found them in my beds and in my cupboards!" shouted one woman.

"They're eating all the food in my shop," called out a vegetable-seller.

"The bread is being eaten before I can get it on my shelves!" called a baker. But still the council

had no ideas. What could
they do?

3

   As the crowd continued to talk, a stranger walked up to them. He made his way to the steps of the town hall where the Mayor and the councillors stood. He was a very curious sight. His outfit was striped yellow and red. He wore a hat with a bright red feather on the side. A long cloak flowed behind him, and he wore short boots with long, upturned toes. The crowd opened before him.

"I can help you rid your town of rats," he said in a very quiet voice.

"Pardon me?" said the Mayor, looking at the stranger before him.

"I said that I can help you get rid of your rats," repeated the stranger.

"You!" said the Mayor. "What can *you* do?"

"I can get rid of your rats for you," he replied.

"But how? On your own? It's impossible!" declared the Mayor. "Pay me a thousand guilders,"

said the stranger, "and I shall rid Hamelin of all the rats."

"A thousand!" said the Mayor. "We'll pay you two thousand! Three! Ten! Just name your price if you promise you can get rid of these dreadful rats! If not, they'll be the ruin of us and our town!"

"A thousand guilders will do. I promise I can rid your town of the rats," said the stranger. "But you must remember your promise to me."

"Of course! Of course!"

declared the Mayor, and the councillors behind him nodded enthusiastically. "By the way, what is your name?"

"People call me the Pied Piper," said the stranger, and he turned away.

The Pied Piper walked
to the edge of the crowd,
and out from beneath his

cloak he pulled a pipe. It was a strange looking pipe, long and thin with many holes in it. He put it to his lips and began to play. A curious tune wafted in the breeze, and was carried through the town. Anybody who heard it was convinced it spoke of big, fat, round cheeses - as big as the moon; fresh crusty bread - tasty and hot from the oven; corn still on the cob - just cut from the stalk! It spoke of all the delicious things the rats enjoyed eating.

The stranger paused,

and the tune could be heard echoing through the houses, shops and buildings of the town. He began to play again, and the towns-people listened hard.

There was a faint whispering sound to be heard from the houses. The whispering grew to a skittering and a scattering. There was a clattering and a rattling, a chattering and a bustling!

A rat appeared - then two! Then four! Ten rats! Twenty! Hundreds, then thousands of rats ran out onto the streets of Hamelin!

They ran from the merchants' houses and warehouses, from the shops and buildings in the streets, from the library and even from the town hall!

The Pied Piper turned on his heel and began to walk down the street. His pipe seemed to be calling out to the rats - Follow me! Follow me! I can take you to a place where there is plenty of food! Follow me! And the rats followed - they could smell the golden cheese and crusty bread the tune promised!

The Pied Piper walked on, with every single rat from the town of Hamelin following him, down the streets of the town and out of the town gate. The towns-people watched from the gate, listening to the tune as it faded into the distance.

He continued down the road leading to the river, the wide River Weser. But the rats did not see the river, they saw a great stream of honey! The tune told them the river was made of honey and that it would be delicious!

The Pied Piper stopped, but continued to play his tune. The rats did not stop, but kept on running! Every single rat jumped into the Weser, believing it to be made of honey, and not one of them was seen again.

5

The Pied Piper stopped playing, and put away his pipe. He walked back to the town and to the square in front of the town hall. The Mayor and the councillors were shaking each other by the hand, congratulating themselves on having got rid of the rats. How clever they were!

The townspeople were chattering, laughing and smiling, delighted to be rid of the rats. Life could return to normal at last! The Pied Piper walked quietly

through the happy people and up to the Mayor.

"I have come for payment of my fee," he said to the Mayor, stopping in front of him.

The Mayor turned to look at him. "What fee?" he demanded.

"My thousand guilders," said the Pied Piper softly.

"What thousand guilders?" laughed the Mayor.

"The thousand guilders you promised to pay me for getting rid of your rats," said the Pied Piper.

"You played a tune on your pipe, the rats liked it and they followed you!" declared the Mayor. "You were then able to lead them to the river. No tune on a pipe is worth a thousand guilders! Anybody could have played a tune on a pipe, and would not dream of charging a thousand guilders for it."

The Mayor had been regretting his rash promise to pay such a large sum. After all, a thousand guilders was a lot of money and it would have to come

out of council funds. There were already huge bills to pay for the damage caused by the rats. The Mayor's chair had to be repaired, for one!

"Does this mean you are breaking your promise and will not pay me my thousand guilders?" asked the Pied Piper.

"You must understand..." said the Mayor. "We cannot afford such a fee!"

The Pied Piper said nothing, but turned away. Again he walked through

the crowd, who were still happy and laughing. He stopped at the edge and turned to face the streets and houses. The Mayor followed to see what the Piper would do. He had a worried look on his face.

6

The Pied Piper took the pipe from beneath his cloak again and began to play. This time the tune was happy and bouncy, magical and playful. It trickled through the streets of the town like a stream. It laughed and gurgled over the houses, schools and buildings.

'Who can it be for?' thought the Mayor puzzled. 'The rats are gone. There's not a single one left.'

Then he heard the sound of giggling and skipping, and realised what the Piper was doing. The townspeople in the square were rooted to the spot. They could not move. They turned on the spot and looked on horrified as their children came into sight, skipping and holding hands.

The Pied Piper continued to play, calling to all the children of the town of Hamelin. His tune sang of happy things - toys and games, cakes and ice creams, holidays at the seaside, days fishing by the river, birthday cakes and party games!

The younger children were carried by the older ones. They had left their schools, returning home for the babies as soon as they heard the music. No child was left behind. They sang and laughed as they came

down the streets to the square.

Their parents could only watch.

Again the Pied Piper turned on his heel, and he led a happy and singing procession down the street towards the town gate. He played his cheerful tune, leading the laughing children down towards the river, the wide River Weser.

The townspeople could at last move, but only as far as the town gate. They watched from there, fearing that their children would suffer the same fate as the rats. But the music continued, and the Piper did not stop. He danced and capered up to the edge of the river, then suddenly turned to the right.

The townspeople watched. Promises of so many lovely things were carrying the children along, and they continued to follow the strangely dressed Piper in front of them. Their parents sighed with relief as they all turned and followed the Pied Piper along the bank of the River Weser. The Piper led them on, through the fields and up into the hills.

At last he came to a cliff, and he stopped. He carried on playing the mag-

ical tune on his pipe, and a door opened in the rocks. The children laughed and skipped their way through the doorway, passing the Piper as he played his tune. When the last child had passed through the doorway disappearing from sight, the Pied Piper followed them. The door in the cliff closed silently behind him.

All the children of Hamelin were lost on that day. The townspeople were very sad. Their children were never returned to

them. The town of Hamelin was a much sadder and quieter place from that day on.

Did I say all the children had disappeared? That is not quite true. Only one child did not go through the magical doorway. A little boy of ten returned to tell the people what had happened to the other children. He was lame, and could not keep up with the Pied Piper and his friends.

He had tried so hard to run with the children. The music of the magical pipe had promised such wonderful things! If only he could run as fast as all his playmates! He could taste the ice cream and the birthday cakes! He could feel the sand beneath his feet and hear the sound of the sea! The ball he wanted for Christmas was his!

But the mountain door had closed before he arrived. He had watched the last of the children disappear, as he tried so hard to catch up with them, and then the Pied Piper had followed them in. The little boy had called and shouted. He had hit the rock with his walking stick, asking to be let in to such a wonderful land, but the door did not open again.

He returned to Hamelin, and had told the townspeople what had happened to all their children. The Mayor and the councillors and all the townspeople vowed never to break a promise again. The price was too high.

And the children of Hamelin were never seen again.